MY CURVY PUCK

C.H. JAMES

GOLDEN STORM PUBLISHING

My Curvy Puck – A Hockey Sports Romance Series – Book One

Paperback - First Edition

Cover designed by Golden Storm Publishing

CHAPTER ONE

HAZEL

The bell of the coffee shop chimes above my head. A smashing wave of heat blasts against my cheeks, making my skin prickle. I gaze around the bustling cafe, tucking the wind-blown strands of my long, auburn hair behind my ear.

She must be here somewhere…

I pull my heavy jacket off, shaking through a shiver. I hang my coat on the stand by the front door. I pull my gloves off and tuck them under my arm just as two tall, bulky men walk in behind me and smile. They reach over my head with their coats and hang them up beside mine. I smile back and notice they're both wearing the colours of the Vancouver Vikings, the local ice hockey team. It's no surprise, the Vikings are the lifeblood of this town.

A warm feeling heats my tummy. It's good to be home.

Vancouver, Canada.

Yes, it might be fucking freezing outside. I'm wearing at least six layers. And that doesn't include the two pairs of less-than-desirable panties I threw on, both of which do nothing to compliment my already huge backside.

But as the two gruff, handsome, rugged men find a seat in the café, crashing on their chairs with a thud, I can only smile.

They don't make men like that in New York.

There's no sign of a suit here. No slicked hair and flashy gold watches.

Nope. It's pure Canadian muscle. And beards. Lots of beards.

Not that it matters to me. I wouldn't have the guts to talk to any of these men if I wanted to. I'm twenty-eight years old and I've barely even looked at a naked man, let alone touched one.

I take a timid step forward, seeking out my best friend. I haven't seen her in three years. I moved to the Big Apple to join a start-up cybersecurity company. I'm now acting as the Operating Officer, and it's consumed my life. Ellie, my best friend, is the reason I took the job, and when I see a flash of dark chocolate brown hair, shining as glossy as I remember, I move towards her.

"Excuse me." I step up to the counter and mock a stiffened expression up at the menu board on the back wall. "Do you serve real coffee here? I mean, what is a Jim Morton's anyway?"

I see Ellie's green eyes look up from the steaming coffee machine. A lazy, uninterested expression meets my gaze, but when our eyes connect, the mug of milk she's steaming drops to the floor and she's dashing around the counter and into my arms.

"Hazel? Hazel!" Ellie bounces in front of me, gripping my top with a firm handful as she hops up and down on the spot in front of me. "You're here! You're really here! What are you doing here?"

I laugh and ignore the fact that the entire café is staring at us. "I'm here for the weekend. Just thought I'd come and surprise you."

"Babe! You should have told me!" Ellie settles down and I can finally get a good look at my best friend. She looks well. Her glowing skin is impeccable, and the plump lips that all the boys fussed over are as chapped as I remember. "Come. Sit. We have so much to talk about."

I look over the counter to a man in an apron who's raised his brows at Ellie. He's wiping at the spilled milk while muttering something about 'lazy girl' under his breath. "Ah... Aren't you supposed to be working?"

Ellie flaps a hand. "Old Geoff will be fine."

Not feeling entirely comfortable with how 'Old Geoff' is looking at me, I follow behind Ellie to a booth beside the window. It's foggy and there's a few used coffee mugs grouped to one side. I sink into the chair and look over at the husky men that walked in behind me. One leans back in the chair, his thick arm draped to one side. His shirt lifts up as he does so, revealing a tiny amount of bare skin, and suddenly my insides come alive.

Without realizing, my tongue swipes across my lips and I can't look away from his curved ass as he shuffles in his chair. His denim jeans are worn at the knees, tassels hanging in multiple threads. I feel my hand grip my leg hard as I stare at the mound in his crotch, picturing in my mind what it might look like beneath. I wonder how it would taste. How it would feel against my tongue...

"Ummmm... Hello?" Ellie waves a hand in front of my face, pulling me from my daydream. "Could you wipe the drool from your lip and talk to me please? I fucking miss you!"

I shake my head. "Shit. Sorry. I didn't real-"

"Realise you were practically rubbing yourself while you looked at Parker?" Ellie pins me with her green eyes.

"Parker?" I ask, my brows scrunching.

"Parker Phillips. Plays for the Vikings..." Ellie looks over her shoulder, and as she does, the bulky man flashes her a smile and waves. "Please tell me you still watch hockey."

Ellie waves back and I get the feeling the players on the Vikings hockey team are regulars here.

I'm not going to lie. I haven't watched a game of ice hockey since the Stanley Cup finals series two years ago. The truth is, I've been too fucking busy working. Ever since the brains behind the start-up company fell ill eighteen months ago, all I've done is work. Getting us to a point where we can start competing with the best in the business has taken a lot of work. Eighty-hour weeks sometimes.

But to sit here and explain that to my best friend, a proud Canadian and the most passionate Vancouver Viking fan?

I've got more chance of finding a polar bear on Main Street. And despite what you might think about Canada, that's just not going to happen.

"Uh… Yeah, I do. I just haven't had much time lately…" I shrug.

Ellie gives me a pointed look, her brows rising. "How's it all going, anyway? What are you doing again? Computer hacking or something?"

I chuckle. "Close. Except the opposite… We're the ones preventing the hacking."

Ellie laughs and clicks her fingers at one of the waitresses. This is a colleague of hers, but Ellie does what Ellie wants. I know that better than anyone. With a wave of her hand and a cheeky smile, Ellie signals for a cup of coffee and then leans back in the chair as if she's got all the time in the world.

"Aren't you getting paid to work right now?" I ask.

"Yeah. Pretty sweet, hey?" Ellie laughs, but when I give her a look, she sits straight again and reaches out for my hand. "Relax. This isn't New York, babe. Welcome back to Canada."

She's right. It is different here… It's fucking perfect.

The young waitress brings over two mugs of coffee. Ellie grabs one and starts sipping, exhaling a loud 'ahhhh' with each slurp. I've missed my best friend's carefree nature. As I sit opposite her, I can literally see her glowing. Her face is alive. She's smiling. Her head and mind are clear. There's no pressure to perform or heavy expectations. She doesn't have a scary CFO to report the less-than-ideal monthly figures to.

Instead, Old Geoff has taken over making coffee's while she kicks back and drinks one for herself.

"The coffee shop gig is still working out for you then?" I try to hide the jealousy in my voice, but something in the way Ellie has pricked up tells me I've failed.

"Yep. It's perfect here. It's easy. I pretty much choose my hours and if I want a day off, I just take it." Ellie throws her dark hair over her shoulder and takes another sip. When she swallows, she looks over the mug with narrowed brows. "As a matter of fact, what are you doing tonight?"

I shrug. All I had planned for my two-day whirlwind trip back home was a quick visit out to my parent's new place on the outskirts of the city.

"Nothing…" I say.

"Good. Noah is playing at Viking Stadium tonight. Come with me."

Noah. *Shit.*

Noah Edwards, Ellie's twin brother, is *the star* of the Vancouver Vikings. He's the biggest, the toughest and the most sought-after hockey player Vancouver has produced in years. He's already knocked back multiple big money offers from teams in the United States. Like his sister, he's Canadian through and through.

And he's fucking gorgeous.

Having a best friend with a hunk of pure Canadian muscle for a twin has always been difficult. For the best part, I found the best way to avoid Noah's smoky grey eyes and well-cut biceps was to keep as far away as possible from him. As you can imagine, that's a bit difficult when you're his sister's best friend. I'd spend all my free time with Ellie, and their family was so involved with hockey that being with Ellie often meant time at the hockey rink.

But Noah was a gentle giant.

At least, to me he was.

Maybe it was because of my friendship with Ellie, but he always looked out for me at school. I was teased and picked on for my size. Being a bigger girl, the 'popular' girls had an issue with me being so friendly with Vancouver's hottest rising star. He was for their eyes only. Only pretty girls get the sexy hockey players… Not chubby chicks like me.

But Noah didn't see it that way. He stuck up for me on countless occasions.

A funny fizzling bubbles in my gut at the memories of Noah, but just like I always did, I shove it back down.

"I don't have a ticket, though…" I say.

Ellie rolls her eyes. "I am the star players sister… I think I can sort you out."

Just as I begin to nod, I see the two guys stand up. My eyes are instantly pulled to them, and again, without knowing, my tongue is flicking around inside my mouth. They strut past, their powerful aura silencing the café instantly. As they collect their coats, Parker winks at Ellie and she twinkles her fingers in a flirty wave.

Ellie spins back in her seat and looks at me, catching me gawking at the firm asses of the two Viking's players. I shift awkwardly, shrinking under her judging gaze.

"Love life going well then?" Ellie says, sporting a smug grin as she sips her coffee.

"Yep. Fine, thanks." I look away, avoiding her amused glare.

"Liar." Ellie shuffles forward. "Out of all the sexy guys in New York, please tell me you've banged at least… I dunno… Like a hundred of them by now?"

Zero. Big fat zero.

I feel the walls of the cafe closing in around me. My mouth dries up and there's a desire to press myself against the freezing cold window just to cool myself down. I avoid Ellie eyes, doing anything to stop myself from looking at her. I start twiddling my fingers around each other, and I feel about an inch tall as I sink into my chair.

"Babe?" Ellie looks down her nose and I shrink even further. Her eyes widen, and I can see the sudden realisation written in her expression. "Oh. My. God… You're not… Are you?"

I bite my lip, still looking anywhere except at Ellie. But this is my best friend we're talking about. She pulls me back in with a snort of her nostrils and a wild slap in the table.

"Please. Not here." I lean across the table, begging with puppy-dog eyes. But I know it's useless. When Ellie focuses in on something, she doesn't let go.

"You're still a virgin?" Ellie gasps and my jaw clenches, warning her to lower her voice. She leans in close, her heavy breath heating my face. "You told me you'd give it a proper shot in the big city. You promised me you'd put yourself out there more..."

"And I did..."

"Oh, really?" Ellie crosses her arms over her chest. "And how did you do that exactly? Let me guess... Photocopy guy thought your tits were too big for him?"

"No... I just-"

Ellie puts her hand up, silencing me. She's shaking her head and I know the look she's giving me. It's the same one she had when we went on our first trip to Vegas together. She's got a plan, and just like the male-stripper to the hotel room shenanigans at Planet Hollywood, I don't think I'm going to like it.

"After the game tonight, you're coming to the locker room with me," Ellie says. I open my mouth to speak, but again I'm left gaping as Ellie interrupts me. "I saw the way you were looking at those guys. Trust me, once you see them in the locker room, shirtless, battered and bruised..." Ellie shakes her body like a jolt of electricity has just flowed right through her. Her eyes are wild with excitement and lust, and I can't help but laugh. "Wow! Trust me bitch, you'll be clambering all over them."

It's completely normal for Ellie to insult me mid-sentence, so it's nice to see nothing has changed there.

"Can't I just come to the game and watch like a normal person?"

"Tell me, Hazel… Do 'normal' fans get to hook up with sexy hockey players?" I shake my head and Ellie's glossy lips curl. "That's right. This weekend… This is the weekend you lose your virginity."

I smile, and when Old Geoff calls out for Ellie to finish her impromptu break, she leaves me sipping at my coffee by myself. I stare out of the window, and my eyes drift to a poster across the street.

'Vancouver's Favourite Viking' is styled in bright yellow typography on the bottom of the poster. After a group of teenagers pass the poster on the wall, I'm left staring across at an image of Noah Edwards, my best friend's brother, gripping a hockey stick with no shirt on. His muscles are cut deep into his stomach, and the low-riding jeans expose the v-shape running diagonally from his hips, pointing me exactly where every woman in this town wants to go.

One weekend to lose my virginity, hey?

CHAPTER TWO

Noah

Holy shit. It's really her. Hazel is really here!

"Noah! Fucking hell! Get with it!" Miles Johnson, the captain of the team, screams at me.

I glance up at the scoreboard. Two minutes to go. We need a goal or we're going to overtime. Again.

I've played my worst game all season. I can't concentrate.

From the moment my sister called out to me in the warmup, I've been on another planet. Not because she was here. No. That's normal. I swear Ellie loves this fucking team more than I do. If we lose this game, she'll feel it more than I ever have.

No. It's not her distracting me.

It's the curvy bombshell next to her. *Hazel Marie Harris.* I can almost feel the warmth of her soft cheeks from the ice. She's a few rows back, and there's a protective glass shield and at least a hundred angry Canadians between us, but her scent floats through the cold air of the stadium, soothing me like a magic potion.

I grip my stick, looking through the wires on my helmet, I search for the auburn hair of my sister's best friend. There was a moment in the second period when I was staring up at her blue eyes when I swear the clock stopped.

I couldn't believe it. *She's back.* An excited flutter filled my body, but it was short lived.

A piece of advice? Don't ever let your guard down on the ice. I stopped skating for two seconds, and before I knew it, I had a fist to my gut and my jersey pulled up over my head.

I'm Noah Edwards.

Last season I was voted the hottest prospect since the man himself, Wayne Gretzky. I was recruited to the Vancouver Vikings on my twelfth birthday, and I made my debut as a skinny seventeen year old. Now, I'm MVP of the league. But with that title comes a giant fucking target above my head.

Oppositions seek me out. It's their job to take off my head. If they can't beat me on the ice, they just beat me. It's that simple.

I'm the lifeblood of the Vancouver Vikings. And I'm the reason we're undefeated this season.

Until now.

"Honest to God, if you don't move your fucking ass, I'ma come over there and shove that stick up your ass!" Miles Johnson screams at me from his position as goaltender.

I slap the top of my helmet and narrow my eyes. A wild roar echoes around the rink and the clock ticks down to the final minute of the game. The crowd are standing, fists throwing wildly in the air, cheering for their team to get over the line.

I bite down on my mouth guard.

Get through this and you can go and talk to her.

"Yes! Parker! Here!"

Parker Phillips looks up. He sees me and passes the tiny black puck my way. I control it with a delicate touch of my stick. My hands pulse against the wooden handle. I can feel the vibration of the chanting crowd. It wills me on, and I look up to see a pair of wild eyes coming my way.

"Not today," I grunt.

I tense my body and hunch over just as the opposing defense-men charges me. He puts too much of his own weight forward, and I notice. *Bad move.* I flick him over my shoulder, sending him face first to the ice with ease. A wild ovation fills the stadium, and I can see shirts and scarves flying around in the stands.

I look across the ice. A clear path to goal has opened up, and I push forward on my skates.

"Ten! Nine!"

I block out the crowd. My lungs are exploding as I gasp for breath. My eyes fix on the goaltender. He's big and bulky, only allowing the tiniest of spaces for me to steer the puck through. He's been fucking brilliant all game. Save after save after brilliant-fucking-save. But enough is enough.

I race forward.

"Five! Four!"

I'm one on one with the goalie. My wrists work the puck side to side, my heart thumping against my chest as I draw to within inches of the goal. This is my moment. This is what I live for. Hockey is my life and that's why I'm the fucking best in the league. I show it week in week out, and tonight is going to be no different.

Especially when she's here.

"Two! One!"

Pulling my stick back, I eyeball the goalie and smile. I whack the puck with my stick, steering it past him and into the net.

"GOOOOOOOOOOOAAAAAALLLL!"

The team piles on top of me as the buzzer confirms the win. That's ten in a row. A league record and guarantees playoffs this year. But somehow, tonight, all of that seems insignificant.

I race down to the locker room, slapping high fives for the kids wearing a replica jerseys with my name on the back. The boys around me are buzzing, chest bumps and manly bear hugs filling the hallway outside of the change rooms.

I push past, finding the locker with number sixteen on it. I sit down in front and remove my skates. There are a few more slaps to my head with excited teammates overjoyed with the victory. I'm bruised and a few cuts sting as the sweat rolls down my cheeks. A beer is thrown to my lap after I remove the protective tape I wrap around my wrists, and when I look up, I feel my insides constrict in a way that they haven't done for the past three years.

"Good win, dipshit," Ellie says. She's got a can of beer in her hand and as she holds it out for a cheers, I look past her to the most beautiful sight I've ever seen inside the Vikings changerooms.

"Hazel?" I say, my voice croaky.

Oh god dammit. She's fucking amazing.

I should crack the can of beer and slurp it down in one, because the nerves rising up my throat are making my fucking mouth dry.

I've spent the last two hours on the ice, dodging seven-foot men with sticks and clenched fists, hatred in their eyes and wishing I was dead, and not once did I feel scared or threatened. But now, as I sit in front of Hazel Harris, my body is shaking so bad I can't even do what a gentleman should do, and stand up to greet her properly.

"Oh, yeah... *Hello Ellie... Thanks for coming to cheer me on...*" My sister's voice splits the air, but I barely notice.

"Hey Noah..." Hazel says, her voice like an angel has come down from heaven and kissed her lips. "Good game out there."

"Ah, thanks," I shrug.

I shift nervously on the bench. Ellie's gawking around the changerooms, and luckily for me, she doesn't notice me taking in her best friend's gorgeous curves. Hazel's just staring down at her toes, and when Ellie looks back to her, she snaps back to me and looks down at the unopened can of beer in my lap.

"Are you going to drink that, or can I have that one, too?" Ellie says, and when I look up at her I see her cheeks are flushed in the same way mine do when I've had a few too many beers.

"Do you really need it?" I say, pinning my sister with a hard look.

"Do you really deserve it?" Ellie says, her brows rising. "You played like shit, bro. What was with you tonight?"

I love my sister. She's my blood and nothing will ever change that. We're tight and it's been that way for as long as I can remember.

But she's also a pain in my ass. She's my number one fan and my harshest critic, and though I should be grateful for that, sometimes it gets on my fucking nerves.

"Fuck off," I say, instantly grabbing at my mouth and looking at Hazel. "Shit." I wince. "I mean! Argh!" I shake my head, hiding my embarrassment.

You shouldn't swear in front of a lady. Not in moments like this anyway. There's a time and a place, and this certainly is one of them.

"Sorry, Hazel."

Ellie frowns and looks at her friend with a scrunched look. I feel my heart rate increase as Hazel chuckles, the sound of her laugh making my fingers tingle and my insides burst with happiness. I look up at her through the tops of my eyes, gazing up and down her body, taking in her generous curves in a way that has my dick twitching.

I've got everything a man could ever want. I make tonnes of money. I play hockey for a living. And I'm so famous that I can't walk in downtown Vancouver without being hassled every two minutes by a fan begging for a signature.

But with Hazel standing before me, her auburn hair sleek, smooth and flowing below her shoulders, all of that feels unnecessary.

"Oh, look! There's Miles Johnson!" Ellie says, her eyes searching the room like they always did when the boys started to hit the showers. "And he's shirtless. See." She waggles her brows to Hazel. "I told you it was good down here. Come on, I'll introduce you."

Ellie grabs Hazel's wrist and begins to pull her in the direction of my captain. I feel the sudden urge to reach out and stop Hazel from leaving, but it's too late. They're halfway across the locker room before I can even mumble a word, and when Ellie reaches Miles, her hand is rubbing his upper arm in a way that makes my lip curl into a snarl.

At least it's not Hazel rubbing him.

I breathe a deep sigh and collect my towel from my bag. With a final glance over at Hazel, who's now laughing alongside my sister, I hit the showers.

I crank the steam right up. My mind is already foggy with the return of Hazel, but I need to clear it out. I played a terrible game tonight. My focus was all over the show. And if we're a chance to get to the Stanley Cup playoffs, I need to be on my game.

I let the hot water run down my back, allowing my thoughts to drift. I replay the game in my head, just like I always did. Only tonight… It's different. Instead of repeating misplaced passes or thinking about my stick technique, flashes of deep cleavage and thick legs distract me. A pair of crystal blue eyes flicker across my mind, and when I look down, I see a raging boner pulsing and begging to be relieved right here in the shower.

"Yo, Edwards?" A voice yells out in the shower room causing me to jump.

"Yeah?" I say, looking down at my hard on, hoping to hell the guys don't choose this moment to play one of their dumb tricks.

"I'm heading out with Ellie…" It's Miles. He's always taking my sister out, but she swears there's nothing going on there. I don't have a problem with Miles, he's a top guy. But I just hope she's careful with him, especially after seeing how red her cheeks were tonight. I know she's had a lot to drink. "You coming to the bar?"

"Yeah, bro. I'll meet you there once I'm done in here."

I look down at my cock and hear the door slam. If Ellie is going to the bar, surely that means Hazel would be too? And dammit, if Hazel is going to be at the bar, I need to make sure I've got a clear mind.

"Well, buddy," I say quietly, looking down at my throbbing length. "Let's get this under control."

With flashes of Hazel's cleavage serving as stimulation, I don't last long before white ropes of pleasure shoot on the wall of the Vikings shower room. *Shit.* Guilt pulls at my neck for the sticky hot mess smoothly flowing down the tiles. I wouldn't want to be a cleaner here. Those are the poor bastards who should be getting million-dollar contracts, not me.

I dry myself down and pull on a pair of underwear before heading back out. Thankfully, my head is clear and even if Hazel is at the bar tonight, I know after my shower exerts, I won't be a mumbling horny mess like I was half an hour ago.

As I turn the corner, the room is much more subdued. The wild cheering and buoyant screams are gone, but the smell of sweaty jerseys and old jockstraps remains. Most of the guys would be halfway to the bar by now, so when I throw the towel over my shoulder and make my way around the bend, I'm left gaping at the beautiful woman sitting in front of locker sixteen.

"Hazel?"

CHAPTER THREE

HAZEL

"Hey, you…" I say, smiling.

Oh god… Oh god… He's naked.

I can almost feel my eyes popping from my head. It's even better than the poster I saw from the window of the coffee shop. My heart is hammering inside my chest, and I can't stop my eyes drifting.

Noah parades across the messy locker room and stands in front of me. He's not wearing anything. Well, at least in my mind he isn't. A white towel pulled over his shoulder and a pair of tight black underwear doesn't leave much for my imagination to figure out.

I swallow hard. Six foot plus of broad, firm muscle. Toned skin gripping shiny muscle upon muscle. Across his chest is a scar that's at least four inches in length, running horizontally. There are tiny droplets of water teasing me as they roll down his abdomen… The lucky towel draped over him has obviously missed a few spots.

Please, allow me…

I feel my centre moisten and my fingers curl.

"Where did everybody go?" Noah's deep voice fills the silent room. At least, I think it's silent. I can't tell. All I'm worried about is the fact that Noah is moving across to sit down beside me in nothing but his tight black underwear.

"They… Uh… Uh…" I clear my throat. "Bar. They've gone to the bar."

"And Ellie just left you behind?" There's a slight annoyance in Noah's voice, and I'm not sure if it's a normal sibling thing, or if there's more to it.

I shrug my shoulders. "Yeah, the tall dude… The goaltender?"

"Miles?"

"Yeah! Him! She went with him… Are they-"

I go to ask the question that's been bugging me ever since I walked into the changerooms. Ellie was drawn to him instantly, and when we went over, it's like I became invisible. But something in Noah's expression changes, and the burning need for more information disappears.

"Nevermind," I say, waving a hand. "Anyway, they took Miles' car. I assume it's something pretty fancy, because he said there's only two seats?"

Noah flicks his brows up and shakes his head. "Yeah. It's fancy alright. And he didn't pay a dime for it. Sponsorships are good like that…"

"Oh, right… Lucky him."

"Damn. They're not messing about tonight then, eh? You can always tell when we have a good win." Noah drags the towel down and rubs it across his chest. My teeth clench together, and I ball my hands to stop them from reaching out and doing it for him. "So, you're back in town then?"

"Hmmmm…"

I purr, lost in another world.

From the corner of my eye, I can see the patterns of his tattoos, intricate artwork inked down the length of his left arm. Noah looks at me, his brow scrunching so his smoky grey eyes squint, making me realise I'm sitting there, practically drooling over him.

"Yes! Yes…" I say, the words coming out louder than I expected. "I'm back. Only for the weekend though. It was a push to get two days off."

Noah stands and begins rummaging through his sports bag. He's bent over and the close-fit nature of his briefs are leaving nothing to my imagination. I can see the huge bulge in the front of his pants and without realizing, my legs are parting. My fingers edge closer to my centre and my lips tremble as I struggle to look away.

"Ellie tells me you're doing pretty well in the big smoke…" Noah plucks a shirt from inside his bag and pulls it over his head, killing a piece of my soul as he does. "I've always been useless with computers. I just bought a new one. My media manager says I need to be more active on the socials… Whatever that means."

I giggle and when Noah looks at me, there's a sparkle in his eye that I've never seen before.

Cut it out, Hazel. This is Noah. He's not interested in you.

Noah finishes getting dressed and after watching him spray cologne over his neck, he spins and looks at me. I feel like a little girl on the locker seat, butterflies running wild inside of me.

I'm staring up at a huge sports star with nothing but admiration. This giant man was out on the ice an hour ago, smashing into incensed titans disguised as opposition players. But he's a behemoth himself. He might be dressed in a smart button up shirt and pressed black chino pants now, but I just saw what's underneath that neat layer of packaging.

Scars. Bruises. Wounds.

It's all there. I've known him for years, but Noah has grown up. He's a man now. Not only that, but he's a damn superstar.

And it's making me fucking wet.

"Right," Noah says. "You're coming to the bar?"

I'm not sure if he's asking me or telling me, so I just nod and stand.

"I guess so," I shrug.

We walk to the door of the locker room, and when we approach, we reach out simultaneously for the handle. As I grip the cold rounded knob, a warm hand glides across the back of mine, clutching at the same doorknob.

Heat splits my hand and the spark between the slight touch makes me pull my hand away as if I was shocked by an electric bolt. I look up at Noah. His eyes are as wide as mine, and he's looking down at the palm of his hand. I wonder if he felt it too, or did the electric shock pass through me and into him?

Whatever it was, I step back, and Noah yanks the door open. He holds his arm out so I pass through first, sucking in a breath of his citrusy scent as I do. I feel his presence behind me, and in the back corridors of Viking Arena, all I can hear is Ellie's voice, echoing in my head...

"This weekend, you lose your virginity..."

***

"Another cider?" Noah asks, his eyes gleaming. "Come on, you have to try and drink from the horns..."

I laugh and shake my head. "I'm not drinking from one of those things!"

I look across to the couple beside us. A bulky man, his beard as full and tangled as I've ever seen, is lifting a horn-shaped flask to his lips. This is a hockey themed bar, and the most popular place in Vancouver to celebrate when the team wins. The brawny fan gulps down, and the beer-filled horn rises as he tips. The woman next to him is holding one, too, her bright red Vikings jersey matching everyone else sitting along the bar.

"And you call yourself a Viking…" Noah teases.

"I never said that," I say, raising my brows playfully. Noah gasps and his mouth hangs open until I slap his arm. "OK! OK… I'm a Viking. I love them. I love them *so much*…"

Sarcasm drips from my lips and Noah crosses his arms across his broad chest. He narrows his smoky gaze to me, and I push down on the warm feeling flushing my cheeks. His lips curl humorously, and when end up laughing uncontrollably together. Something inside me twists at the sound of his chuckle. It's deep and raw. It's untameable and rough.

I've spent the last hour telling myself he's not interested, so don't even bother. So what if he's bought all my drinks since we sat up at the bar? And just because he's ditched his teammates to sit with me… That doesn't mean anything.

Does it?

Noah waves his hand at the bartender. There's a line up for service, but when the bartender sees its Vancouver's favourite son waving at him, he's pouring fresh drinks for us instantly. He whips over with two freshly poured pints of warm cherry cider, in glasses, not Viking horns, and leaves with a wink directed at Noah.

"Wow… It must be nice being a famous hockey player in Canada…" I say, holding my glass for a cheers.

Noah clinks my glass. "It has its perks."

Ellie's here somewhere. She's attached at the hip with that hockey player, and as her best friend and knowing her like I do, I know she's smitten with him. Searching the room for my friend, I feel a pressure in my belly, and I know I can't hold it in any longer.

"I need to go to the ladies," I say.

"I'll wait here for you," Noah says, and when I rise to my feet, he rubs my upper arm with a soft caress. "Don't *pee* long…"

I roll my eyes at the terrible joke and force myself to make my way across the bar, my arm still burning from Noah's touch.

The floor area of the bar is packed with bodies. Music is pumping from a jukebox in the corner, a few couples dancing in circles in front of it. A wave of people sporting red hockey jersey's light up the orange glow under the lights. There are drinks spilling and splashing to the sticky floor, as crazy fans celebrate the last-minute win of their favourite team long into the night.

I smile.

It's good to be home.

I reach the dark corridor that leads to the ladies room and take a glance back over my shoulder to the bar. A blonde girl is moving in and hoisting her tiny frame onto the bar stool I was sitting on seconds ago.

My stomach sinks. My ribs feel like they're pulling in tighter, restricting my heart from beating. My body sways on the spot and I gulp down, suddenly needing the wall to uphold my balance.

"Hey babe!" A cheerful voice beams from behind me, causing me to jolt on the spot.

I look to see Ellie's bright eyes sparkling. Her lipstick is smudged and as I look over her shoulder, Miles is strutting up the corridor behind her, adjusting himself at the front of his trousers. He stands behind Ellie and reaches down, fondling her in an area I don't want to know about. She jumps on the spot with a squeal, her eyes popping. My expression hardens, and as it does, Ellie smacks his hand away from her backside, looking at me with a stiff smile.

"Everything ok? Is something wrong? You look like you've seen the Vikings lose..." Ellie says, lowering her concerned gaze to me.

"I'm fine..."

I'm lying. I'm not fine.

I glance back across and the blonde has her hand running down Noah's arm. She's smiling, her teeth so white I can see the glow from where I'm standing. She's tilting her head and giggling. Her hair is flowing smoothly down her body, and the low-cut top has a giant 'V' stretched right across the bust, making her perfectly shaped breasts pop.

She's everything I'm not. And Noah seems to like that.

"I've got to go to the bathroom," I say, and push past Ellie and Miles. She's yells something out, but it's a blur and I don't really care right now anyway.

Idiot. Fucking idiot.

I lock myself in the cubicle and takes deep breaths to stem my scattered breathing. My heart is racing, and I pace one step back and spin, repeating it over and over while slapping my palm against my forehead.

I shouldn't have let myself believe it. He's Noah Edwards for fucks sake. As if he'd ever be interested in taking my virginity? He's not interested in me. That wasn't flirting. I'm his twin sister's best friend, he was just being nice. She ditched me so he filled in and that's all there is to it.

"ARRGGH!" I scrunch down and scream.

I'm a fool for wanting him anyway. It was never going to happen. I mean, look at him. He's a famous hockey player. He could have any woman. Hell, he could have any man he wanted, judging the way some of the guys in this bar were looking at him... So why would he want me? A plus-size chick with thighs wider than Ontario?

Not only that, but what would Ellie think? It's part of the best friend rulebook, isn't it? You don't date your friend's brother. It's forbidden. It's distasteful. It's wrong!

I pull the door open and drag my feet to the sink. Leaning down, I splash cold water over my face. I catch my sad eyes in the mirror and shake my head.

"Just go home..." I whisper to myself.

CHAPTER FOUR

NOAH

One of the worst parts about being a professional hockey player in a place like Vancouver, a city that literally lives and breathes hockey, is that you can't go anywhere without being hassled.

"And the way you handle that stick…" The blonde in front of me flutters her lashes in a way that I've seen a million times before. "I can only imagine what else you can do with your hands…"

I nod and smile, not really listening, but being polite, nonetheless. I'm searching for Hazel, but the bar is reaching peak capacity. It's nearly midnight. The crowd inside *The Bloody Viking* are getting rowdy and it's at about this time that I usually go home.

But I'm not leaving without her.

"… and then she said that you can increase the size of them even more… What do you think?" The voice next to me begs for attention, but my neck is craning, my eyes scanning every inch of the bar.

And then I see her.

My gut pulls and I'm launched from the bar stool without even knowing I meant to do it. Bony fingers curl around my shoulder, pulling and tugging… begging me to come back. But I pull away from the girl and her plastic chest. The crowd in front of me parts like I'm freaking Moses and I push across the room.

"Hazel!" I call out, but the bar is so loud even my deep voice doesn't reach her. Her auburn hair is swishing as she walks hastily towards the green exit sign. "HAZEL! HAZEL! HAZEL!"

I feel like a pathetic puppy dog. But I don't care.

Where is she going?

I thought it was going so well. Ellie had been too busy doing whatever the hell it was that she had been doing, so I had Hazel all to myself. We'd been laughing, having fun and I even caught her looking me up and down a few times. I'm no Hugh Hefner, but I took that as a good sign.

I'm trying to stay focused on Hazel, I can't lose sight of her otherwise she'll disappear into the crowd of bodies. A large guy in a Vikings jersey, and yes, of course it has my name on the back, is steaming across to me. He's going to try and stop me for a photo, I just know it. He's just got that longing, desperate look in his eyes. They're popping from his head, but I can't stop now. Not tonight.

I reach in my pocket, plucking my wallet from my pants. Taking big strides across the room, the rough man starts yelling out.

"Edwards! Edwards! Yo, EDWARDS!"

I pull a card from my wallet and look at him. He's standing in front of me, his mouth almost on the floor. He's got grey hair, what's left of it anyway. This is a grown man… He'd be at least my father's age, and then some.

But he's fangirling like crazy, and to this day, I've never let a fan down yet.

"Here," I say, grabbing him by the shoulders. I shove the card in his chest, and he grabs it. "That's my agent. Call him and we'll go out for a dinner." I step back, leaving him staring at the card, his hands shaking. "Or… I'll get you a corporate box for the playoffs. Or… A signed jersey! I'm sorry, I just… I just… I have to go!"

I stumble backwards on someone's leg behind me. I take a second to regain my balance. When I look over at the exit, I see the door swing open, and a bounce of silky, velvety hair blows from the wind gushing through the door.

I race forward, grabbing the door just as it closes. It's fucking freezing outside, but the pain prickling my hot cheeks is nothing compared to the twisting in my gut right now.

"Hazel?" I call out to a vacant, snow-covered street. There's a few drunk men smoking just outside of the other entrance to the bar, and another drunk man stumbling up the street singing 'We Like To Party' to himself. Steam rises from vents on the sidewalk, and aside from the bass of the music blaring from the bar, and the drunk man's fading rendition on the Vengaboys classic, it's silent.

I'm not letting her go. I've waited too long for this.

I look down. Crunched snow shows footsteps that lead off in all different directions. There's too many to follow a particular one, but a flash before my eyes has images of Hazel's burgundy Dr Martens boots resting on the bar stool. I couldn't get enough of the amazing curvy goddess as we sat at the bar. Every chance I got, I gazed up her gorgeous legs and took in her thick, juicy-looking thighs. I wanted to split them. I wanted to see what was between them and taste it.

But that won't be possible if I don't find her.

I crouch down, feeling like a Park Ranger in the mountains as I scan the various styles of imprints in the snow. I begin to lose hope, but then I see it…

"There," I mutter, looking at an imprint that's rounded at the back, wide at the front and a gap in the middle. "Boots. Hazel's boots."

It looks fresh and I follow them. This is a big city and despite spending the last two hours with Hazel, I stupidly didn't find out where she was staying. *What an idiot.* She could be on a bus for all I know, heading to her parent's place on the outskirts of the city. I've been there once before when we dropped Ellie off after a hockey try out, but that was a long time ago, and I'll be fucked if I remember exactly where it is.

I follow the footsteps, my breath coming out in heavy steam from my mouth. A few minutes pass and the steps get softer.

"I'm close," I mumble.

My chest bounces and I'm panting hard. I spend most of my life working out, but the nerves building inside of my body are making me feel ten times heavier than normal.

And then I see it.

The bright lights of *Vancouver Inn* shine like an oasis in the middle of a desert. The deep crevasses of boots in the snow lead right up to the reception and I race ahead, my head thumping.

I burst through the front door, ignoring the glowing gaze the bellboy looks across at me with. I've already promised one fan something I might not be able to follow through with, I can't make another one.

The bright lights of the reception desk shine in my eyes. I squint, the glare a stark difference to the darkened streets of midnight in Vancouver.

"What do you mean there's no booking? I have the confirmation right here!" A sweet voice rings through the air and my heart gives a leap inside my chest. "Look! It's right here. *Hazel Harris. Two nights.*"

"I'm sorry, Miss. It's not in our system." A deeper voice replies.

I step forward, culling my pace to a slow walk.

"Well can you just find me a different room then please? It's late and I just want to go to sleep…" I see Hazel from behind. She's leaning on the counter, bent over so her backside is protruding invitingly. I stare for a moment, feeling a twitch in my pants before it's cut short by the man behind the desk.

"Like I said, there aren't any rooms left." His tone has changed, and when he looks from his computer screen, he looks down at Hazel in a way that has my fists clenching. "What part of 'no rooms left' don't you understand?"

My nostrils flare and I race up behind Hazel, slamming my clenched fist on the counter.

"Good evening." I feel my lip twitch as I spit the words out at the receptionist. He shrinks down under my presence. I can see he's recognized who I am by the way he's looking at me. I don't look at Hazel, but there's a burning on the side of my face that tells me she's staring up at me. "My friend here has booking that you need to honour…"

Hazel shifts on her feet and her scent has a calming effect on me. My cheeks are still burning hot, but having her by my side again soothes the adrenaline ripping through my body.

"Um… Uh… Sir?" The man stutters, avoiding my eyes. He's a fully grown man, but standing across from me, shrinking to the floor like he is, he looks like a little boy, wishing for his mommy to come and save him. "We don't-"

"The emergency room. She'll take it." I demand.

"E-e-emergency r-room, sir?"

"Yes. She'll take it."

The man looks over my shoulder to where the security is standing. He gives them a wide-eyed look and then nods.

I've been on the road and stayed in enough hotels to know that no hotel is ever 'fully booked'. In case of emergency, there's always a spare room. And as far as I'm concerned, as Hazel stands beside me, her eyes tired and her legs struggling to support her tired body, this is the biggest emergency I've ever fucking seen.

There's a tapping on the keyboard behind the desk, and after a few silent minutes, the man pulls a set of keys that look almost brand new from a drawer and slides them across the counter.

"Level sixteen. Room one."

I smile and grab the keys. As we turn, Hazel reaches down to a case that I hadn't even noticed was beside her when I stormed in. Rage had skewed my vision, tunnelling it so I could only focus on the prick who was speaking down to my girl.

My girl? My girl?

"No," I grunt, frowning at the gorgeous girl before me as her hand clasps around the handle of her suitcase. "Leave that. Please… allow me."

Hazel smiles up at me, and an odd flicker in her eyes tells me that she's surprised to see me. We move towards the elevators, walking in silence while her boots clop across the glossy tiles. I smile to myself, a warm feeling in my tummy making me feel fuzzy inside as I see the burgundy boots that led me back to her.

CHAPTER FIVE

HAZEL

Breathe. Just breathe.

I push the key in the door, but my hands are shaking wildly so I struggle to work it all the way in.

"Here…" Noah places a hand on my shoulder, and I sink into his touch. He moves around, grabbing the keys and gliding it in with the calmness only a professional athlete could exude. "There we go."

His voice echoes inside a tiny hotel room. I stand, glued to the spot.

The opened door smashes back against the wall. Without stepping inside, I can see the back wall of the room from the corridor. There's a double bed pushed against the wall and either side of the bed is a modest bedside table, each topped with a dimly lit lamp.

"Wow…" Noah ducks under the doorway and hunches over as he steps in the room. I giggle to myself, and he looks back at me, his face amused. "What are you laughing at?"

"You look like a giant. Either that or you've shrunk the room…" I say, catching my laugh with my hand.

"Hey, be quiet!" Noah chuckles, his chest bouncing. "I got you this… this… Well, I guess it counts as a room…"

Noah looks around, his brows pulled in a twisted expression.

I poke my head in the door and to my left, there is a tiny bathroom. There's a toilet and the smallest shower I've ever seen, but I can't see the sink until I push the rolling door back.

"Well, the council has been saying that space is tight in the CBD for some time now…" I shrug. "I guess we should have listened shouldn't we."

Noah steps over and although he's smiling, I suddenly feel my body tense up. I still can't believe he's here in front of me. The second I heard his firm tone from behind me in the lobby, my ovaries clenched up and they haven't released since.

It's his smell.

It's his looks.

It's him…

"Why…"

I hesitate, my finger pulling at my lip, wondering whether I should ask the question that's burning my tongue. Noah inches closer, and even though the room is tiny, I feel like he's crowding me.

But in the best way possible.

"Why what?" Noah asks, his husky voice a whisper.

"Why did you come after me?"

My body's trembling. I dodge his hungry eyes, unsure what the hell he's doing. This is Noah Edwards. He was just at the bar, chatting with a stunningly beautiful woman. She was his for the taking, and fuck, even as a woman, I could see that she was a stunner. What kind of man wouldn't be back there with her right now?

I look up. To my amazement, Noah's smiling. His eyes are soft and gentle. The beefy man from downstairs is gone. The raging hockey player I saw on the ice tonight has been tamed. His authority has evaporated and all that's left is this gentle giant before me.

He's holding doors and carrying my suitcase. He's demanding hotel rooms for me and he's not taking no for an answer.

That doesn't mean anything, Hazel.

"I couldn't let you walk in downtown Vancouver late at night all by yourself, could I?" Noah's moving in closer. He's licking his lips, but surely I'm imagining that? My stomach clenches as his breath touches my lips. "A beautiful woman like you… Alone in the dark?"

"Uh, yeah, I guess... Thanks?"

My throat feels thick. The tiny hotel room closes in around us, and when I take a step back, my ass hits the wall. Noah advances.

"Hazel," Noah breathes, and his palm smacks against the wall as he leans over and traps me under his gorgeous muscle-soaked body. His breath is stifled, and his pupils are growing. "Hazel... I'm going to say something I've been holding onto for a long time. I'm tired of fighting inside my own head. Day and night. Over and over again..."

I'm pressed hard against the wall with Noah towering above me. His chest is pressing against mine and the heat radiating between our bodies is sizzling. My eyes blink rapidly, almost as if they don't believe it either.

"I want you."

The words leave his mouth and work their way through my brain and down to my lips. Without thinking twice, I throw my hands around his neck and my mouth is attacking his.

"Oh, fuck..." Noah gasps, his hands dropping and gripping my hips. "You're kissing me. Holy shit. You're kissing me!"

I detach, my breath heavy. "You want me to stop?"

Noah chuckles and I feel his hand pull me in the centre of my back.

"No way."

I crash into him, our mouths a mess of wild, wet smothered chaos. Noah pulls me up, so my legs are forced to wrap around him, and with the strength of an entire army, he's holding me against the wall. He splits my mouth with a swipe of his warm tongue, demanding entrance.

I clasp his cheeks with two hands, my tongue working inside his mouth, devouring his taste like it's the last time I'll ever kiss someone.

It might be the last time I kiss Noah. Noah! Noah fucking Edwards! I'm kissing Noah Edwards!

"Oh, baby…" Noah pulls back, his hungry eyes dropping to my wettened mouth. "Oh, fuck you taste so good…"

I grip his shaggy hair and force him back to my mouth. My body explodes with desire. The tiny hotel room seems a distant issue now, instead, the air surrounding me is steamy like a sauna. A hot, vicious wave of pleasure rises in my stomach, shooting off in all different directions around my body. Noah works his way down my neck, pecking and nibbling my sensitive skin. My nipples are hard against the fabric of my bra, and I feel the wetness in my panties flood against my swelling pussy.

"Noah…" I gasp between smothered kisses. "Noah…"

"Yeah, baby?"

I groan, not wanting to say it. But I have to. She's my best friend and he's her brother. *Twin* brother at that.

I let him bite down on my neck for a few seconds longer. If I'm going to kill this passion before it evens get the chance to burn, then I want to enjoy every tiny second I get. Noah sucks my collarbone and my head rocks back. My eyes roll, and involuntary moans leaves my chest.

Noah lowers me back to the floor and the second my feet hit the ground, he's grabbing at my rounded ass, squeezing so hard tingles of pleasure pulse through my core. I don't want this to stop, but I'm a good friend. I'm a damned good friend, and that should always come first.

I scrunch my face tightly and let the words I know I'm going to regret leave my lips.

"What about Ellie?" I say, forcing another kiss before he can answer and possibly put an abrupt end to this forever.

"What about her?" Noah says, sliding his tongue inside my mouth again. We kiss before I manage to pull back from this hungry beast.

"She's your sister… She's my friend…" I say, my breathing coming out in short, sharp bursts. Noah leans in to kiss me again, but I will the courage to pin him with a pleading look. "Please, we need to talk this through before we do something stupid…"

Noah releases his hold on me and takes a small step back. He lets go of my body, leaving me stranded and cold in front of him. He looks me up and down. The hunger that was there only moments ago has suddenly been… satisfied?

"Well?" I say when Noah just stands there, not offering a word for what feels like forever.

"Hazel…" Noah's voice is gentle, but there's a stiffness to it that he's never had with me before. "When we were at the bar tonight, where was Ellie?"

My forehead creases. "Um, I don't know. With that guy... Miles or whatever his name is."

Noah nods and a tiny smirk appears. "That's right."

I feel an ache in my belly and I know it's my body's way of telling me I'm a fool. But I don't understand what he's getting at. So what if Ellie was with Miles? What's that got to do with anything?

"Yeah..."

"Miles is my oldest friend. He's been there for me since I started at the Vikings as a twelve-year-old kid. He was nineteen, and he had just started making senior appearances on the team."

I listen carefully, but as much as I try, I don't get it.

"But, Noah... Miles and Ellie... You don't even know if anything is-"

Just as Noah pins me with raised brows, guessing exactly where I was heading with the next sentence, my mind casts back to the bar. I had just seen Noah with that girl, and because my mind was a mess, I must have fogged over the groping hands of Miles when I ran into Ellie outside of the bathroom.

"He's your best friend." I announce and Noah confirms with the smallest of nods. "And she's your sister." Another nod. "But that doesn't make it right. Two wrongs don't make a right, didn't your mother ever tell you that?"

Noah laughs. "She did. She also told me that you should chase your dreams and desires. If you want something, you stop at nothing to go and get it." Noah moves in closer, and when his hands wrap around my waist again, my stomach gives a grateful flutter.

Maybe he's right?

I've done my dues. I've waited my turn. I'm a twenty-eight-year-old virgin. I work all day and my social life is non-existent. I've never put myself first, even with the cybersecurity company I bust my ass for all day long.

Well, fuck. Maybe it's time I think of myself first for once.

I lean up on my tiptoes, lifting my lips to meet his. A delicate smile patterns out across his face and the cheekiest little grimace makes my heart leap.

"You think you're pretty cute, don't you?" I say, smiling.

"Meh." Noah shrugs, the smirk growing. "I've never been told otherwise."

He leans down and presses a kiss to my lips. "I can't believe I'm kissing Noah Edwards…" I say. "The famous Noah Edwards."

He smiles. "Why can't you believe it? I didn't do a very good job of hiding how much I wanted you, did I?"

"Well, I didn't know!" I say, my eyes widening. "When I saw you with that girl…"

I see Noah's eyes widen and there's a realisation spreading across his face. "That's why you left… Back at the bar. You saw her talking to me."

"I saw her rubbing your arm and puffing her chest out at you, yes…" I say, my voice coming out firmer than I anticipated.

Noah pulls me in tighter, wrapping his arms all the way around my body. It's like I'm a teddy bear and he's a scared child. He's holding me so closely until the fear passes. Only, when I look up at him, it isn't fear in his eyes...

It's... It's...

No. I'm not going to say it. It's stupid to even think it.

"Hazel, you didn't have to run away," Noah says, pressing his forehead down on mine. "I was never going to ditch you. That woman was nothing compared to you."

I scoff. "Ha! Are you kidding?" I say. "What? The perfectly round boobs and hourglass figure not your type?"

The smirk returns again, and for a look I've never seen on him before, twice in two minutes is almost too much.

"What?" I gasp.

"No. She's not my type." Noah pins me with a broad smile. "You're my type."

I feel his firm crotch pressing into me and all I want is to reach down and grab at it. I can feel the size of it against my leg, and the throbbing bulge is teasing me with a torment like I've never experienced before. Just as that thought crosses my mind, another one comes along and sends it smashing back up the tracks.

I have to tell him. If tonight is going to go where I think it might go, then I have to tell him my secret.

"Um," I whisper, so quietly that Noah leans in closer. "There's something I should tell you…"

Noah's eyes widen and he seems to stop breathing. My heart is pounding inside my own chest, but I know this is something I need to own.

"What is it?" Noah's deep voice is barely a whisper, but it still fills the room despite his attempt to lower it to a soothing tone. His eyes are kind, but concern pulls at them. "Hazel… Whatever it is… You can tell me. You can tell me anything."

I swallow hard.

"I'm a virgin."

CHAPTER SIX

NOAH

"Y-y-you're a virgin?" My voice is suddenly husky.

Hazel lowers her shrunken gaze to the floor. My chest is tight. I'm struggling to breathe, and it feels like I'm in the third period of a play-off game and we're down by two goals. The pressure has just doubled, and it sits firmly on my shoulders.

"Yep. A virgin." Hazel's talking to her feet with a distant tone that's far, far away from the hotel room where we stand.

"Oh, wow…" I whisper.

Hazel takes a step to the side, leaving my grasp and makes her way to sit on the edge of the bed. Her body is limp, almost lifeless, as she remains still with her back hunched.

A shaking feeling fills me.

But does this really matter? I'm feeling things for this girl that I haven't ever felt before. This is Hazel. So what if she's a virgin? In fact, even better. No man has ever been there, so I can take her as mine... If she wants, or permits, me to.

Something rises up my stomach and forces my lip to stiffen. My brows crease, and I close the space between us. I kneel on my knees in front of Hazel. Her wet, regret-filled eyes remain stunningly beautiful, and my tiny smile greets her gloomy expression.

"I'm not going to lie..." I hold her hands, gripping them tightly. "This changes everything."

I see the searing rip tear through her heart. It pains me to watch as Hazel's chest heaves and she's holding back the tears that swell her eyes. She doesn't say anything, but she's nodding with an acceptance that her secret *is* a big deal.

"I lost my virginity when I was sixteen..." I begin, and Hazel huffs a snort.

"This isn't the time to brag..."

"I'm not bragging, sweetheart," I say, pulling her eyes to mine with a soft smile. I draw a breath, trying to calm myself down. "My first time... It wasn't special. It's not something that I think about that often. As a matter of fact, I haven't even spoken to the girl for years. I don't know where she lives... Or if she's happily married with kids and a husband. I know absolutely nothing about her."

The room is silent, and I feel every deep breath Hazel takes. Her eyes glisten under the yellow hue of the budget light fitting above us and it's killing me knowing that I'm the one making her feel this way.

I can see this means something to her. But it means something to me, too. I *felt* it. I'm still feeling it. Christ, that kiss? Wow. I've never had a kiss like that.

"The night I had sex for the first time was just a normal night for me…"

Hazel pushes on her knees, impatience forcing her up. "Well, congratulations on years and years of hot, meaningless sex. You must be proud of yourself." Hazel tries to escape my clutches, but I pull her hands so she crashes back on the bed.

"I'm not proud. That's not what I'm saying."

"Then what are you saying, Noah?" Hazel's voice rises and her eyes change. "Spit it out."

I grip her hands tightly, they're soft and smooth and I never want to let them go.

"Hazel…" I whisper and lift her chin with one finger so her eyes meet mine. "I want you… I want you more than I've ever wanted anything before in my life. But it needs to be special. After what you've just told me, that's the least you deserve."

I look around the minuscule room. The bed is rock hard, the blankets stained and tattered. There's paint peeling on the wall and there's barely enough room to sit down, let alone have sex in here.

"Wh-what do you mean?" Hazel stutters.

"This room… This is no place for a queen like you to blossom her flower for the first time…"

Who the fuck just said that?

The words leave my mouth and I'm as shocked as Hazel at the poetic nature of them. But that's what this woman does to me. She's not like the other girls I've been with. Hazel does something to me that no one else has ever done.

I look at her and I see a future. I see love and passion. I see… I see the beginnings of a family of my very own.

"Come with me." I shoot to my feet and, still grasping Hazel's hands, I snatch her case and steam out of the room.

"Where are we going?"

"It's a surprise. Just relax and…" I turn and stop so suddenly that Hazel's perfect body crashes into mine and our faces are almost touching. My face is hardened, my eyes serious when I say, "Just trust me."

Hazel nods. It's a firm, resounding nod that I know means she trusts me completely. She looks at my lips and choosing not to waste another damned second, I lean forward and press them on hers.

The kiss is deep. The fuse locks our mouths together, and every desire floating inside of me doesn't want to pull away. But there's better things to come, and that thought helps me pull away.

"Let's go." We force ourselves apart. If only for a moment. "I have a plan."

★★★

I scatter the red petals over my bed. I've already changed the sheets to the best and softest fabric I've got, and the crisp whiteness of the Egyptian cotton makes the roses petals pop. The candles on the bedside tables wave gently, flickering a soft light that matches the scent of velvety smooth vanilla.

"Hmmm…" I grip my chin, deep in thought. "Too cheesy?"

I shake my head.

She'll love it.

I glance at the clock on my wall. I've left Hazel on the sofa in my living room for too long. We'd barely muttered a word on the ride back to my place. I was off in another world, planning everything in my head. And Hazel? I think she was just a nervous wreck. I mean, she was about to lose her virginity to her best friend's twin brother. If that doesn't make you nervous, then I don't know what will.

But I've got a plan. I'm going to make this night the best damn night of her life.

And then some.

She'd be halfway done the bottle of wine I cracked for her by now, but maybe that's not a bad thing?

I take one last look at my bedroom and an excited jump makes me spin and hurry to collect the girl I've wanted to do this with for years.

"Are you ready?" I call out.

Hazel's bright face turns from my lounge. She's gripping a glass of red wine, and to my surprise, she's barely touched it. I step across and pick up the bottle, studying the nearly full contents and raising my brows to Hazel.

"I want to remember it…" Hazel shrugs, answering my questioning frown.

I smile and nod, and after placing the bottle back down, I hold my hand out, inviting Hazel to link up with me.

"Come on," I say. "It's ready."

Hazel's hand clutches mine and I lead her down the hallway. My legs feel like jelly, and when we reach my bedroom door, I step back and allow Hazel to push the door open. Nerves streak through my body. I'm well known for holding my nerve on the ice. But right now… my hands are shaking like I'm about to be smashed by a pair of seven-foot tall defensive backs.

I've never done anything like this before. I scrounged the candles together from the bottom drawer in the kitchen. I'd used them in a blackout once before. The rose petals? A stop at the gas station on the way wasn't a complete waste after all, was it?

Please like it. Please like it. Please like it.

I won't lie. I'm packing it.

But the sight of the bedspread glowing under candlelight has Hazel twirling into my arms, her mouth attached on mine the second she catches sight of the scene I've set.

"Noah…" Her lips push onto mine and I pull her in tight. "Oh my god… You did this just now? For me?" Another scattering of wild kisses tingles my cheeks. "I love it. Thank you. Thank you. Thank you!"

Hazel is on her tiptoes, her arms pulling around my neck, so I'm forced to kiss her. But that's no issue. I devour her, inviting her to part her lips with a swipe of my tongue. She opens wide, permitting entry and our breath intensifies.

"Wait…" I say, pulling back for a second. "There's one more surprise…"

"What?" Hazel kisses my neck, and her hands are gliding down underneath my shirt.

"Go and get comfy on the bed," I say, breathless already. "I'll be back in a second."

Hazel frowns, but I push her backwards, guiding her to crash down on top of the rose petals. Dozens of petals shift around her falling body and I step backwards. I watch Hazel every step of the way until I'm in my bathroom, closing the door so she can no longer see me.

I change quickly. Stripping down and then dressing again. I adjust my new outfit as fast as I can. My cock is already firm, and the black g-string I've just thrown on isn't permitting much room to move. I grab the bottle of oil I had hidden away in the bathroom and slide the door open again.

"Good evening, Miss," I say, deepening my voice. "Are you the fine lady who ordered a massage?"

Hazel giggles, her mouth gaping at my new outfit. Her eyes lap up every inch of my exposed skin, making my cock rise higher as it throbs and twitches. When I throw the oil bottle up in the air and fail to catch it, she's laughing so loudly that my heart drifts across the room and attaches to her, never to leave again.

Chuckling, I move across, grabbing the massage oil from the floor as I do. The feeling of my hardness pressing against the silky fabric of my g-string is turning me on even more. I tap the edge of the bed, inviting Hazel across. She crawls over, her crystal blue eyes drinking in my bare chest. I flex hard, liking the way she's licking her lips as her hungry gaze crawls over my abdomen. A warm hand drapes across my toned midsection, sending a blistering warmth through my body. I gently pull at her shirt, lifting it over her head to reveal a deep red bra.

"Turn around," I whisper, craning into the crook of her neck and sucking gently.

With a quick press of the hook, her bra comes loose. She turns back and I gasp at the sight of her generous curves. I crouch down at the edge of the bed, and she shuffles forward, allowing me to draw a nipple in my mouth.

"Oh… " Hazel moans the second my tongue touches her.

I remind myself to take it slow. This is her first time. I can't rush this. But with the way she's enjoying herself already, I don't think I'm going to have any trouble easing her in.

Her peaks are stiff in my mouth, and I drop to oil bottle to the floor and cup the other breast. "Oh, fuck… Your tits are perfect." I groan, swiping my tongue across her delicious nipples. I pull her up, undoing her jeans and sliding them down before lowering her back to the edge of the bed. "And your legs… Oh God, how long I've wanted to see between these gorgeous thighs…"

My hands guide her legs apart. She's laid back on the bed, her arms laying either side of her head as she relaxes in the ambient light of the flickering candles. I wonder whether I should have added music to the scene, but when I see the moisture flowing beneath the wet fabric of Hazel's moist panties, the thought disappears instantly.

"I want to taste you…" I say, leaning up on my knees. My cock throbs and it's all I can do not to reach down and rub it. "Lift your hips for me, baby…"

I slide Hazel's panties off and my insides burst with anticipation. "Oh, yes… Yes, Hazel. Gorgeous, beautiful Hazel…" I can't stop staring at her glowing pussy. She stays quiet. This is new to her, and I remember how shy I was about being vocal in the bedroom. "Relax, sweetheart… Let me take care of this for you."

Gently, I rub the tip of my finger against the swollen hood of her clit. She's wet. So wet, it's dripping. A murmur of pleasure whimpers from above me, and I wet my lips. "I'm going to taste you…" There's a moan of permission and I refuse to waste another second.

A growl leaves the back of my throat, my eyes drink in Hazel's soaking pussy. My mouth is on fire, demanding me to dive in headfirst – literally. But I will myself to ease forward smoothly. Slowly. Her legs quiver, and as my tongue touches her, her hips lift from the bed, and I see her hands grip the fresh white sheets with a scrunched fist.

"Ohhhhhh…" Hazel's moaning and struggling to keep her hips grounded. Her hand grips my hair and I press my tongue firmly against her clit, circling with each hard grip she tugs on my hair. "Oh, fuck… Yes… Oh, God."

I work my tongue faster, lowering to her entrance and dive as far as my tongue will go. My hands work the insides of her thighs as I explore her pussy, nipping and nudging with my mouth. I don't have to do much before Hazel's fully relaxed, and that's when I work a finger inside her.

"You're so fucking tight…"

I know she's a virgin… But fuck me. She's tight. Really tight. So tight that my index finger works slowly inside her, guided only by her body language. I tease her with my tongue, lapping her clit as I push my finger deeper, her opening allowing me slowly further inside. I feel her tensing and I know she's going into the promised land.

Has she ever orgasmed before?

"Oh… Shit! Oh, that feels good…" Her words, mixed between deep moans, echo off the wall of my bedroom. Boy am I fucking happy this isn't that pitiful hotel room. "Noah… Noah… Yes!"

A smirk meets my lips. This woman is loving my touch and it spurs me on to work harder. Hazel's hips are grinding my finger, and when she leans up on her elbows, eyeballing me from above, I know she's there.

"Yes! Yes! OHHHH!!!"

Hazel collapses backwards, her head crashing to the bed with a thud. She's stopped breathing and her body is twisting on the bed. My finger feels like the circulation is cut off. Her entire body contracts and I can almost see the waves of pleasure riding down through her body, starting at her eyes and escaping around the tightness of my finger.

I ease her back from the orgasm, rising to my feet when I know she's finished.

"Roll over," I say, twirling my wet finger in the air. I squeeze oil into my hands and once Hazel's settled at the top of the bed, her face resting in the soft pillows and her bare round ass towards the ceiling, I jump up and swing one leg over her, so I'm straddling her in a backwards way. I squeeze more oil over her bare back, and when she's glossy and slippery, I toss the bottle aside and warm my hands. "Just relax and close your eyes, baby…"

CHAPTER SEVEN

HAZEL

My body feels hot beneath his touch. The soft mattress acts as my platform, cushioning me as I sink down. The darkness of my closed eyes allows me to drift into a world of pleasure. It's a world that I thought was in a far distant galaxy. A place that everyone else except me would get the chance to venture to.

I've been with men before. Not all the way, but on two occasions, and two only, I've felt the touch of a man. Yes, I am a virgin. I don't know whether something about my body scared them away, but I never went all the way with either of them.

Did it affect my confidence? Did I think it was something that I was doing that made them run out before doing the final deed?

You bet your ass it did.

Until now.

The way Noah's touching me makes me feel like I'm a fucking goddess. His slippery hands work over every exposed inch of my skin. He's rubbing, pushing, probing and every now and then, he leans down to my neck and applies gentle kisses. I can feel his scratchy stubble on my shoulder before he nips and bites along my neck.

"Is it ok, baby?" Noah's deep voice catches me off guard.

I nod into the pillow, offering a slight groan for a response.

I'm in dreamland. Surely this can't be real? It's all too magical.

The candles. The flowers. The oil.

I feel Noah's heavy palms press down my spine, tingling sensations following his fingers as they draw lower. He's been working my body over for at least twenty minutes. I've been on work trips to exotic locations where they offer inhouse massages by trained professionals… And let me tell you: they're nothing compared to this.

I feel his warm hands at the top of my ass. He's sliding down my legs and an excited shiver runs down my body, following his warmth. My insides jolt with excitement, and just as his hands press against the insides of my thighs, I feel a squirt of liquid flow from my pussy.

"Oh… Oh my god… You make me feel… So… So…" Noah spread my legs and his hand cups my pussy. He guides my rear up with a gentle hand, so my face is buried in the pillow. His oily fingers circle my clit and I bite down hard. "Oh yes… Baby…"

My voice is muffled in the pillow as my face smooshes into the bed.

I've played this scene over in my head a million times. I'm twenty-eight, and for the first time in my life, I feel confident in my body. Every lump, every curve is on display. But the lighting? The scene that this gorgeous man has provided... He's made it perfect. This is special.

He circles my pussy from behind and when I feel a finger inside me, I'm biting down on my lip. He grips my ass with his free hand, and when he releases, there's a gentle slap that stings my skin.

"Oh!" I screech, the surprise gentle spank of my rear end catching me off guard.

I feel my centre moisten further, and I shake my booty. My full ass cheeks wobble, and I peek through the gap between my arm and my body to see Noah's hungry eyes half-hooded, staring at my curved ass.

"Fuck yeah, baby," Noah groans. "Work it for me. Work it."

He pushes his finger in and out... In and out. He's getting deeper and it feels like there's an itch that needs to be poked, but he can't quiet reach it. I keep my ass shaking, pushing back with my hips to get that itch satisfied. He likes it, and even though it's only my virginity being taken tonight, this night doesn't have to be all about me.

He slides a second finger in, and a shock of pleasure pricks my stomach. I rock back on his fingers, watching him. A weird feeling rumbles beneath my chest as I stare up into his grey eyes.

This is a man that I've known since I started high school. He's my best friend's brother. He's a fucking famous athlete. He could have anyone he wants.

And yet, here I am… Falling in love with him?

Noah catches me looking, and with a cheeky smirk he winks and pushes deeper with his fingers. I moan, my mouth gaping open as I stare up at him. He fucks me deeper, and I look down at the black g-string that's doing its best to constrict him.

I pull my body forward, letting Noah's fingers glide out from inside of me. I scooch around, lowering to his crotch, and pull down on the band of his underwear.

"Your turn…" I say, looking through the tops of my eyes to Noah.

His hand is grabbing the back of my head, guiding me towards his hard on. I yank down to reveal a length that deceives the bulge it was protruding.

"Wow," I mutter, clutching my mouth. "Um, it's fucking huge…"

My hand grabs the girth, wrapping tightly and sliding up so the hood pulls back. A tight vein pulses beneath my hand. Now, I haven't seen a lot of dicks, but this is one sexy cock that's dripping and begging to be tasted.

I open my mouth, shuffling forward to take him. My lips wrap around him, and the feeling is a new one for me. Noah grips my hair with a fist, rocking forward on his knees as he slides his cock against the walls of my mouth.

"Oh, yes…" Noah's groans will me on. I open my throat in a way I didn't know I could, allowing me to take him further in my mouth. I gag on his bulb, the new sensation at the back of my mouth making my wetness drip. "Fuck yeah. And you've never done this before?"

I leave his cock in my mouth and look up at him, shaking my head. He seems to enjoy seeing me with his cock in my mouth, because there's a wicked smile crawling across his chiselled features.

"You're a naughty girl, aren't you?" Noah says, his voice deep and rough. I nod, still with his cock pushed down my throat. It chokes me, but I think I like it… "Wow, no, you're not a naughty girl… You're a good girl. You're a very, *very* good girl."

Noah reaches over my body and smacks my ass. I let out a whine and feel more wetness drip from my pussy. I'm so turned on my eyes begin to blur, either that, or they're watering because I can't get enough of this large, throbbing dick in my mouth.

I whip his dick from my mouth and stroke it fast in my hand. It's long and wet and my hand glides up and down quickly, spreading my saliva and making it all wet. Noah's eyes roll back, and I see the muscles in his well-defined six pack twitching as I focus my wrist on the sensitive end of his cock.

"Noah…" I look up to him, my eyes needy. "I want you. I want you now…"

Noah doesn't need a second invitation. He leans down and grabs me like I'm a feather. He lifts me up and throws me across the bed. All the air escapes my lungs as I watch him crawl across on his knees, his body a rippled mass of muscle, tattoos and old hockey wounds. His eyes are slits, and behind them, there's a lust and longing that no one has ever looked at me with before.

He lowers himself down and reaches across for the foiled packet on the bedside.

"Wait!" I grab his wrist as it passes over my head. "Leave it. I want to feel it. I want to feel you. Properly."

"Are you sure?"

I nod, biting down on my lip. Noah's staring at me, his face hardened. "I've got my contraception under control."

To be honest, I don't know if my contraception works. How would I know? I've never had to worry before. But what I do know is that I want to feel his hot skin against the inside of me. I don't need a protective layer. I don't want *anything* to come between us in this moment.

I've waited too long, and I want the proper experience.

"OK," Noah says. He grips himself and strokes a long fist down his cock. "Just as long as you're ok with it."

"I am," I say. I pull at his stomach, my nails digging into his taut skin.

Noah nestles in between my legs, gripping his cock. His eyes meet mine as he shuffles forward. I feel the tip of his length on the outside of my entrance, and I force myself to take a long, deep breath.

This is it.

I gaze up at Noah. I'm staring into his eyes but all I can hear is my best friend's voice rattling around inside my head.

"Oh my god… You still haven't done it?"

"Out of all the guys you could have slept with…"

"This weekend… This is the weekend you lose your virginity."

"Baby…" Noah's voice pulls me from the trance. He's smiling, his face is bright, and I feel like he's hugging me with those stunning eyes of his. "Are you ready?"

I nod. "I'm ready."

Noah pushes forward, concentration wrinkling his brow. I feel his hardness against my folds, pressing a firm pressure at my entrance. I grab his hips, aiding him as he slowly pushes inside me.

"Oh…" My eyes close without even meaning to. A feeling of new warmth fills my core, a feeling like no other that I've felt before. "Noah… Yes… Noah…"

Noah smiles and I feel him guiding in further. He rocks his hips back and when he moves forward again, my body permits deeper entrance.

"Oh, baby," Noah moans, his eyes latched to mine. "You feel so fucking good."

I nod, holding his frame with a hard grip of his hips. He thrusts with deeper movements. A hunger rolls my insides, a deeper craving for more. Noah collapses on top of me and draws a nipple in his mouth. He sucks hard, leaving with a pop before pushing his full length inside of me.

"OH!" I squeal.

The full feeling inside me has my breathing all over the place. I'm gasping for breath, but I want it again.

"Yes, fuck me…" I demand.

Noah thrusts deep again. A thumb drapes over my nipple and it's like a rod of lightning hits my belly and shoots down to my core. He thumbs it again and without even realizing, my fingers are circling my clit while he's fucking me.

"Oh, baby… Come for me… Come for me, baby…' Noah demands, his eyes now hungry.

He pushes harder inside me, and I can feel it coming. A ball of fire is ignited and it's growing. His dick is long and hard inside of me, but it's smooth as it glides with deepening exploration. I rub myself, the feeling of the top of his dick turning me on even further as a circle myself.

And then everything seems to happen all at once. Noah crashes down, his hardness tensing. His stubble grazes my neck as he nuzzles in, biting down as his hips jerk in rapid movements. The fireball grows inside of me, but it's moving. It's going down… Down…

"OHHHHHH!!!"

"Yes! Oh, fuck… FUUUUCKKK!"

It takes me a second to open my eyes.

My chest is heaving.

My heart is beating rapidly.

There's a warmth oozing from my exhausted pussy.

I glance to my side. Noah's laying there. He's not blinking as his chest rises up and down. He's staring up at the ceiling almost as if he's another world away.

I gulp down.

Shit. Did I do it wrong? Was I really bad at it? That wasn't bad, though… Was it?

After another minute or two of silence, I can't take it anymore. I roll to my side and catch Noah's eyes. They're tired. Exhausted.

"Is everything ok?" I ask, feeling about as big as a pea.

Am I being needy? Is this the after-sex hormones that I've heard about coming through? But he's just laying there. He hasn't said a word since… Well, since you know…

"Babe?" I push again, this time poking a finger into his ribs.

"Yeah, yeah… Everything's fine." Noah twitches against my poking finger. He rolls to his side and faces me. But as he does, a weird expression pulls at his lips, lifting them up on one side, but remaining steady on the other. "Hazel… I…"

Oh, great. This is the part where he makes some dumb excuse and runs out. I'll never see him again.

"I… I'm… I'm in love with you."

CHAPTER EIGHT

NOAH

People think that just because I'm fearless on the ice, means I'm a tough guy in every aspect of my life. I've had journalists, reporters and media personalities shrinking beside me after a game. They're intimidated by me because of my sheer size.

It's not just that.

My temperament before, during or after a big game is one of pure focus. That's why I am where I am. I'm the best in the league for a reason.

But the feeling when you declare your love for someone and you're laying there waiting their response... That's a feeling I never want again.

"Y-you love me?" Hazel's voice breaks the silence of the room. The candles are still alight, swaying in the stillness of the room.

"I love you." I reaffirm it, not only for Hazel, but for myself, too.

I'd always felt something for Hazel. I knew there was an attraction there, but I just thought it was a normal big brother thing... Don't most brothers find their sister's friends attractive? That's normal, right? Right?!

The seconds pass by and it's like my insides have been torn from my stomach, laid out on the bed and she's just biding her time, deciding which organ she wants to crush first.

"You love me?" Hazel says, and I feel like I'm in a fucking vortex, going round and round and round.

"Yes." I say, my voice firming.

"You love me?"

"Yes! Hazel, wh-"

"You love me!" Hazel's voice changes, but I don't notice until I'm sitting upright in the bed. I go to stand; I've got to escape. I'm feeling utterly embarrassed, and until I turn and see Hazel's bright eyes, wide and blue, I want to escape. "You love me!"

"Yes, Hazel," I nod, my brows rising at the glowing look she's giving me. What the hell... Is she stuck on repeat or something? "You can keep saying it, but it won't change what I said..."

Hazel crawls across. She's still naked and her hard nipples glide across my forearm. A rocket shoots through my body, and as she grabs my hands in hers, my goddamn cock comes back to life.

"I don't want it to change…" Hazel whispers. She leans in and kisses me with the softest of kisses on my bottom lip.

"Oh," I grunt, sounding more like a caveman than a pro hockey player.

"Noah…" Hazel's voice is soft and elegant. "Tonight… This…" She waves an arm around the room, showcasing the efforts I put so much work into. "No one has ever done anything like this for me before."

I shrug. "It was nothing. I'd do anything for you, Hazel. You know that."

She kisses me again, only this time, she lingers and pulls my bottom lip in her mouth with a hard suck.

"I know that *now*…" Hazel pulls a finger down my chest. My cock twitches with her touch, and she must feel him bouncing around down there, because she reaches down and grabs it with a thick grasp. "And before you start round two… There's something you need to know, too."

I groan, stopping my eyes from rolling back in my head. She's stroking me, and despite having blown my load five minutes ago, I'm ready to go again.

"What's that, sweetheart?" I say, my eyelids getting heavy. She pulls me harder and I'm doing everything I can to keep my eyes attached on hers.

"I. Love. You. Too."

Hazel pecks a kiss to my lips with each word. With a wave of relief lifting the tension that had been building on my shoulders, I lift her and throw her back.

"Spread your legs for me, baby…" I growl. "Don't you know Noah Edwards is a second period specialist?"

***

"Vi-kings! Vi-kings! Vi-kings!"

I look up to the stands. Ellie's in her usual seat. The stupid fucking red foam finger waving above her head. She insists it brings the boy's good luck. I don't care if we've never lost when she's worn it – it looks fucking ridiculous.

My neck cranes around from the ice. Fans are piling in. Red polo's and replica jerseys with my name on the back as far as the eye can see. The atmosphere is building. Music blares from the speakers on the Megatron.

We're minutes away from puck drop.

And then I see her…

A flutter fills my stomach. Hazel Harris. My girlfriend… Or at least, she will be by the end of the night.

We've talked about it. We're in love. So what if it's only been four days? She extended her stay in Vancouver and I lay claim as the reason for that. She's spent every night at my apartment and she's certainly making up for lost time in terms of remaining a virgin for so long.

But, being the way-too-good-of-a-friend to my sister, Hazel's insisted that before we go any further with our 'relationship', she needs Ellie's blessing.

I smile up the stands and wave. Ellie waves the massive pointing finger glove at me and bounces on the spot. I'm not waving at her, but she doesn't know that. She doesn't know anything yet, at least, I don't think she does. Maybe Hazel has told her already, and Ellie really doesn't care? I mean, why would she? We're all adults, right?

I gulp down.

Beside Ellie, Hazel is smiling, but it's twisted. I can feel her nervousness from here. She's worried about me. She said she doesn't want to be there to see me get hurt.

But I never get hurt. I'm Noah Edwards. MVP. And this ice is mine.

"Vi-kings! Vi-kings!"

The crowd screams and a rumble from the stands vibrates the safety glass that surrounds the rink. I line up, eyeballing my opposing man. I swish my stick in my hand, swapping from side to side as my lip twitches.

I can feel the excitement racing through my veins. The chanting of the crowd eggs me on and my brow narrows at the man opposite me. My entire world might be watching from the stands, and as soon as this game is finished, I can't wait to be safely back in Hazel's arms... But for the next two hours, I'm an angry Canadian again.

"And game!"

The puck slams to the ice and I push forward with the roar of the crowd, my eyes glued on my man. I don't worry about the puck, that can wait. I own this ice, and I'm going to make damn sure these assholes know it.

Skating quickly as the bodies break into formation, I duck down, stiffen my shoulder and close in on my opposite number. With a snide smile and evil laugh behind my helmet, I wink at him and connect my shoulder against his chest, winding him instantly and sending him flying to the ice in the first play of the game.

"Hey, fucker!" His teammates are straight on me as he crashes to the ice. A group of yellow jerseys are shoving me with their sticks and throwing punches aimlessly at me.

A smile touches my lips, as a fist smacks around the back of my head, sending my helmet flying across the ice and a searing pain down my back. I live for this shit. A brawl breaks out before my eyes and when I look up at Hazel, she's on her feet, her face red from screaming. She's loving it and I've never been prouder. Beside her, Ellie's arms pulse through the air, her clenched fists punching wildly with every flying body that collapses to the ice.

Another smack at the back of my head forces me to turn around.

A deep chuckle builds inside of me. The smallest guy on the ice stares up at me, his eyes wide with fear. He's awoken the beast, and he should have picked on someone his own size.

"Oh… little man… You really shouldn't have done that."

I chase after the rookie and pull his jersey back. It yanks up over his helmet and I throw it over my shoulder. He slips on the ice and when I crouch down over him, I shake my head and smile down at his wide, petrified eyes.

"Fuck, I love hockey…"

SMACK.

CHAPTER NINE

HAZEL

"I can't believe you're going home already…" Ellie pouts her chapped lips out.

"What do you mean *already*? I stayed an extra four days than I was supposed to…" I say, lifting the steaming mug of coffee to my mouth and slurping loudly.

"Yeah, but I never got to see you on those days… What have you been doing anyway?" Ellie pins me with a look I know all too well.

She's right. I might have stayed an extra few days, but I haven't seen anyone more than I did in the first two days. No one aside from Noah. Noah and the four walls of his bedroom.

"Well…"

I avoid my best friend's eyes. I can't hold it in anymore. Noah has been patient. Naggy and annoying as he desperately reminded me to just get it over with…

But still patient.

I do adore the fact that he's so excited to finally get the correct label on what's going on between us. For us to be 'in a relationship' means more to him than it does to me. I know what I feel, and I know Noah feels the same. But… I guess I still lay awake at night, confused. Completely satisfied after yet another round of steaming hot orgasms… But confused.

How did I get this man?

I'm an ordinary girl. I'm not pretty or attractive. I'm plus sized and my lumps and bumps are bountiful and endless. I sit behind a desk most days at work, barely afforded the time to scratch myself, let alone have a proper relationship. I go home and microwave my dinner and repeat the cycle over and over again.

But yet, here I am… About to seek permission from my oldest friend to date her twin brother.

"Well, what?" Ellie says. She grabs a glass of water and downs it quickly. Her eyes are sunken and blood shot, but I dare not ask why. "What is it you've been doing?"

I shuffle forward in my seat, my heart hammering inside of my chest. Just as I open my mouth to reveal all, the bell of the coffee shop chimes, and a group of teenage boys walk in. They're talking passionately about last night's game. It was intense and the Vikings dominated the opposition from the moment… well, from the moment Noah sent their Captain flying in the opening seconds.

The guys are noisy, and I see that each of them is dressed in a red hockey jersey, a giant Viking helmet branded on the front. I smile, and as they step across to the counter, I see the name on the back.

'EDWARDS'

And it's the same on all four of the tops.

Ellie sees my smile and follows my gaze. Rolling her eyes, she mutters. "Honestly… My brother could be mayor of this freaking city. He's more popular than the current dipshit who's in charge. Everyone loves him."

My throat thickens.

Noah has been so confident that Ellie won't care about us. But I'm not as confident. I see the way she talks about him when he's not around. There's an underlying jealousy there. It's always been there, and I can even see it as I sit across from her right now.

And on top of that, I'm about to unleash yet more pain by re-vealing *I'm* in love with him too? Her best friend! And not only am I in love with him, but I want to spend the rest of my life with him and have his fucking babies…

Maybe I won't say that part yet. That can wait.

I glance at my watch. My plane departs Vancouver airport in two hours, so I have to get a wriggle on. Security is a bitch as the best of times.

I shuffle forward and reach out for Ellie's hand. When I grab it, she frowns at me in the most 'Ellie' way possible.

I draw in a deep breath and ignore the rising eyebrows of my best friend. "The reason I stayed a bit longer... And the reason that you haven't seen me in that time is because..."

I hesitate, but then I see a flash of Noah's eyes at last night's game. The way he looked at his opposition, there was no fear there. He had courage. He oozed confidence and belief. Noah was a man who saw something and stopped at nothing to get it. He chased me from the bar without me even knowing, and when the hotel shafted me, he stood there and demanded action.

I bite down on my tongue. "Ellie, I've been seeing Noah."

A clattering of cutlery smashes in the kitchen. A barrelling of laughter beams from the table beside us. The teenagers are replaying the goals from last night on their phones, the commentary blaring loudly around the coffee shop.

"You're what?" Ellie breathes, staring directly into my eyes.

"I'm seeing Noah," I confirm. Ellie's expression scrunches and weirdly I feel the need to clarify who I'm talking about. "I'm dating your brother."

I shrink at my choice of words. Ellie's just sitting there, and I can hear her brain ticking over. Any other way of saying it would have been fine. But no, I choose the worst combination possible.

"Please, say-"

"As in Noah? You're dating Noah?" Ellie asks, her voice weird.

I nod. "Yes."

"Oh my god!" Ellie shoots from her chair and throws her arms up like she's got that awesome foam finger back on her hand again. "You're dating my brother! Are you for real, girl? Really? Like actual proper love each other and shit?"

I nod, allowing myself to smile. "Yeah… Proper actual shit."

Ellie darts around the table and pulls me in her arms. All the air escapes my lungs and if I wasn't mistaken, judging by the grip on this girl, I could swear it's the other twin hugging me.

"Oh, this is great!" Ellie settles back in her chair, her hands rolling around in each other. "We'll be sisters. *Actual* sisters."

It's then that her face drops. "Wait a second…" She eyeballs me and her brows pull into a 'V'. "You didn't… Did you? You and Noah? Your…" She leans across the table and cups her mouth. "Virginity?"

I smile and poke my tongue between my teeth. "Gone."

Ellie scoots back and her wide eyes are unblinking. I expected more of a reaction, but I remind myself of the amount of information Ellie is processing right now. "Wow." She pauses. "You're going to get married, right?"

I shrug. "Um… I don't-"

"Oh, you have to get married, babe!" Ellie shrieks. "You just have to. Oh, can I help plan it? Imagine the wedding you'll be able to have! You know he's loaded, right? Has he told you that yet?"

I laugh and shake my head.

Ellie continues on her barrage of hyperactivity, bouncing from one dream wedding scenario to the next. I take the chance to whip my phone out and tap out a text to Noah – I promised him I'd let him know as soon as I had done the deed.

After a few minutes of more mock wedding planning, I look to my watch.

"I'm really sorry, but I have to go…" I push my empty mug to one side and Ellie glances over at the counter. Old Geoff is eyeballing her, demanding she return to work with his fierce eyes.

"I'll take you," Ellie says, pushing up off the table.

"What?" I gasp. "Ellie? You're working!"

"He'll be ok. Plus, I won't see you for another… Well, actually! You'll be here all the time now, right?" I shrug and Ellie helps me from my chair with a heavy yank of my arm. "Well, if you manage to make time for me that is… With all the baby making you'll be doing…" Ellie stops in her tracks and when I look back at her, her eyes are wider than ever. "Oh my god. I just realised. I'm going to be the aunt to your children!"

I giggle and follow behind Ellie as she dances out of the coffee shop with a wave over her shoulder directed at her scowling boss.

Epilogue

Hazel

Three Months Later

I look down at my finger, the diamond glistening as my ass bounces back on Noah's thrusting hips.

"Oh, fuck you feel so good…" Noah pushes inside me further, deepening his grip on my hips.

"Fuck yes, do me, baby…" I push up on my palms so I'm on all fours. The floor of the locker room isn't the comfiest place we've done it, and my knees are stinging from the pain of the hard concrete beneath me. But what better way is there to celebrate the romantic proposal Noah just pulled off than by fucking in the first private space available?

"You take it good, fiancé," Noah groans. He smacks my ass and grips it with a full handful.

My eyes close and I rock back against him as I shake my head. I still can't believe it.

How didn't I see it coming?

I mean, everyone was there... Noah had provided tickets for my entire family. Mom and Dad sat in the same row as us, and Ellie was there with hers and Noah's parents. It was a big game; the playoffs are in full swing and the Vikings are favourite to reach the Stanley Cup. With all thanks going to my man, and lead scorer of the series, of course.

The game was intense, but as soon as the buzzer went to confirm another win, sending Vancouver's favourite team through to the next round, my life changed.

The lights went out. Pitch black darkness gripped Viking Stadium. Jaws theme music started playing and finally, when the lights burst back to life, Noah appeared beside me, hunched on one knee, holding an open box with a dazzling bright diamond ring. He'd removed his helmet, but his jersey, hockey pants and ice skates remained sweaty, torn and sexy as fuck.

The Megatron showed the entire stadium my grinning expression. I nodded like a fucking crazed monkey, jumping into Noah's arms with a gleeful leap.

I feel his cock tense up and I know he's close. The guys have given us the privacy of the locker room, but we won't need it for much longer.

"Yes, baby..." I moan, dipping my head between my arms.

"You want my cum inside you, sweetheart?" I groan a confirmation and Noah's strong hand smacks my ass. "Tell me you want it."

"I want it. I want your cum." I moan, my neck jerking back under Noah's fistful of my hair.

I've certainly been making up for lost time. I might have had to wait until after my twenty-eighth birthday to pop my cherry, but now it's popped… Well, let's just say two hundred and six times is a lot in three months.

I rock my hips and my head rocks back and forth, as if I'm disagreeing, only, I'm doing the complete opposite. "Yes, yes!" Noah steadies and maintains his pace, pushing in all the right spots. I reach down to my clit, it's tightening, and my pussy is starting to flutter. "Oh, fuck. Don't stop! Don't stop!"

Noah growls and I'm so fucking turned on. I glance at the ring, and it sparkles back at me as if confirming I will be getting this treatment for years and years to come. *Bring it on.*

My nails dig into the concrete, and I feel as if they'll scratch the surface. Noah adjusts his position and pulls my hips back, his breath hot and heavy on my back. His cock angles just right, and I feel each thrust deeper and deeper. It's hitting that spot, and I know it will get me over the line.

"Oh!" I'm screaming now, and I don't give a shit who hears me.

"Come with me," Noah growls, his voice rumbling through my body. "Now, baby! Now!"

I release and shriek Noah's name. My pussy convulses around his length and when I feel his hotness filling me, his faces collapses to my bare back.

We relax and when Noah settles down against the bench seat of locker sixteen, I lay my head on his shoulder. Together, we catch our breath. I reach across and thread my fingers in his, smiling up at the handsome man that is my fiancé.

"I love you, Noah Edwards," I smile.

He turns and cups my cheek with his warm hands.

"I love you, too, Hazel. I love you today. And tomorrow. And forever." He lifts my hand and kisses the ring he offered as a symbol of his everlasting commitment to marry me. "You're my soulmate. You're everything to me. And I'm grateful we finally told each other exactly how we feel."

"Have you guys got clothes on yet?" A loud voice comes from down the corridor. "We want to come in!"

I look at Noah and laugh. He reaches behind us and retrieves our clothes. "Yeah, come in!"

I dress quicker than I ever have before, the feeling of Noah's warm cum sitting in my panties as it drips out of me an odd feeling that I never knew would turn me on so much. Finally, when I turn around, Ellie is standing there with her Mom and Dad.

"Oh, Son!" Noah's Mom darts across and wraps her arms around her son. I smile at his dad and when he moves across to congratulate us, he embraces me like I'm one of his own.

"Welcome to the family, Hazel."

I smile at Mr. Edwards. As I go to hug his Mrs. Edwards, my parents steam into the locker room and they're closely followed by a group of huge hockey players, led by Miles Johnson.

Ellie stumbles across to me and wraps an arm around my shoulder. She smiles at me and shakes her head. "I can't believe you're actually getting married. Well done, babe. I couldn't be happier for you."

There's a hint of sadness in her eyes. Does Ellie want what I've got? I've spent my entire adult life wishing to be more like her. Care-free and living life in the moment. But as she stares around the room, I see her eyes lock on Miles. I wonder whether there is more there than what they let us see? Does Ellie actually have deeper feelings for Miles?

I'm pulled from the thought by Noah pushing Ellie aside and pulling me in tight.

"Back off, Sis," Noah says, smirking. "You had your turn. Your best friend is mine now. Mine forever."

"Forever and ever."

I lean up on my toes and lay a deep kiss on Noah's mouth. The entire locker room cheers and chants for the newly engaged couple.

I've never been happier.

EXCERPT FROM THE NEXT IN SERIES

CAPTAIN'S CURVY PUCK - BOOK TWO

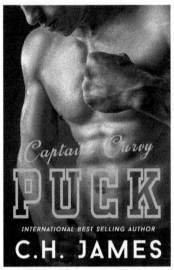

Find it on Amazon or your pre-ferred online book store!

MILES JOHNSON

I pull a deep gulp of my Budweiser, resting the cold bottle on my knee. The television blares loudly in front of me. The darkness of my dim living room makes the flashes of slow-motion replays even more eye-catching.

We fucking did it. Another win.

I take another sip as images of Parker Philips slapping home the fifth goal of the night plays out on the screen. The crowd roars on the TV and the camera pans to our leader, Coach Best. I chuckle, as the screen makes him look even more intense than in real life.

If Coach knew I had downed three beers already, he'd have me skating laps for hours.

I don't care.

I'm thirty-six years old, so I'm going to kick back on a Saturday night and drink a few fucking Buds if I want to.

Don't get me wrong, hockey is my number one priority. It always has been. Ever since I was twelve and I was drafted to the Edmonton Eagles. I made an instant impact, rising quickly through the team to make my senior debut at the prime young age of fourteen.

To this day, I'm still the youngest player to debut at the Eagles.

But when Canada's best team came in for me, there was no fucking way my dad, God bless his soul, would let me knock back the Vancouver Vikings. Not that I wanted to. They offered me big money straight off the stick. I don't care who you are - a few grand a week for a pimple-faced rookie is a lot of money.

And I haven't looked back since.

Four Stanley Cups. Five MVP awards. And my pride and joy, the Olympic Gold medal.

A smile creeps across my face as another goal flies in the back of the net. This time Noah Edwards slaps the puck home from a tight angle late in the third period. The camera zooms in on him, and then quickly pans to the crowd.

A sea of red and white rise from their seats, all clapping and cheering on the TV. I know it's only a replay, but still, a feeling of pride builds in my chest. Being the captain of Vancouver's favorite team is a privileged position. I can't walk anywhere in this city without being pulled aside for a selfie. Even on the rare occasions when I go to *The Bloody Viking,* the famous bar in the city centre, I'm mauled and harassed by drunk men and horny chicks all night.

Honestly, if it wasn't for the foul stench of the fans' breath, or the way the girls rubbed their plastic tits against me, I seriously wouldn't mind the attention.

Could I put up with it every minute of every day?

Hell no!

Why the fuck do you think I'm sitting in my living room on a Saturday night all alone?

But I understand. I'm a hockey fan, too. Even I get all fan-girl crazy when I see Wayne Gretsky and Mario Lemieux at the end-of-season award functions. The first time I met *The Great One,* I was in the bathroom of the Ritz Palace in London. I was so excited that I forgot I was pissing at the urinal and let go of my cock. I peed all over his shoes and ruined a very expensive pair of leather Oxfords.

We joke about it now, but believe me, it was awkward between us for a while.

The last dregs of my beer slide down my throat. The final buzzer blasts, and I watch Noah Edwards pick up yet another man of the match award. That's eleven this season – he's favorite to defend his MVP title, and deservedly so.

I scooch forward in my armchair, pressing my knees to head into the kitchen to fetch a fourth beer. As I feel my knees creak beneath my hands, I'm stopped mid-way by the image of a gorgeous, curvaceous woman on the television screen.

"Ellie…"

The name leaves my lips like a breath of fresh air.

A twist in my stomach forces me to stand tall, my eyes fixed on the screen. Noah's twin sister, Ellie Edwards, is cheering from the stands. Her lips are red and glossy – they look as plump, chapped and kissable as ever. Her dark, chocolate brown hair is as smooth as it always is, shining in the flashing lights of the Viking Arena. I love her hair… The way it flows down her body, long and elegant towards her busting cleavage.

I feel my cock twitch, but before I can reach down, she's gone. Ellie's perfect face is replaced by two men in suits. They're not even close to being as good looking as Ellie. They're holding microphones and talking passionately about yet another impressive win for the Vikings and it's enough to force me to spin around.

I grunt and turn to retreat to the fridge, the image of Ellie's tits stirring inside my head. I reach for the final beer in the coldness of my bare fridge and when I pop the cap, I hear my phone buzzing on the table.

I run back, sucking a deep gulp of the fresh fizz of the lager.

"Hello?" I grab my phone and swipe without looking.

"Miles, bro!" A deep voice shouts, though a mix of background noise is making it hard to hear. "Are you there? Hello?"

"Yeah, I'm here," I say, pulling my phone to look at the screen. I see '*Noah*' as the caller and when I push the phone back to my ear, a loud smash clatters. "Noah? Is that you? Is everything ok?"

"Bro! I can't really hear you," Noah's voice yells, another smash of glass rattling my eardrum. "I need you to come down to the bar. It's fucking crazy here tonight and I might need some help keeping things under control."

I slurp my drink and look down at my comfy black trousers with a deep sigh. I'm also wearing my favorite Beatles shirt. It's the shirt I wear when I want to be comfy. It's my go-to top when I'm sure I'll be laid back on the sofa all night. It's so fucking old the cotton is soft and worn down. It's the softest fucking thing I've ever felt. I don't care if it's faded and got holes in it… It's. Fucking. Comfy.

"Oh, man…" I drag out. "Are you sure you can't handle it? I'm settled in for the night, man."

The phone fumbles and I hear girly screams and deep roars of wild hockey fans. There's chanting and by the sounds of it, someone has one of those Vikings horns and is using it in a sculling contest. Without him even saying, I know where Noah is. There's no other place in the city that has people who makes noises like that.

The Bloody Viking.

It's the place to be for hockey fans.

"Miles! Are you there?" Noah's voice comes back to the phone. "Seriously, I need to go. Some weird chick has straddled Jamie Fisher. Bro, when you get here… Find Ellie."

My stomach drops at the mention of his twin sister's name.

Ellie's there…

"…she's disappeared and I can't look for her." Another fumble echoes in my ear, but I'm already racing up the hallway to change my pants when I hear Noah's final words, "I'll see you when you get here."

I grab the first pair of jeans on the floor of my bedroom. Stepping across to my wardrobe, I pluck a white hoodie and race out of the front door of my apartment, only stopping to slide on the closest pair of shoes to the door.

One of the benefits of being a pro-hockey player is I get paid handsomely. I can afford a downtown apartment, and as I sprint up the dark streets of late-night Vancouver, I've never been more grateful for that.

I turn the final corner and my chest heaves at the sight of at least thirty bodies loitering outside of *The Bloody Viking.* You know it's a busy night when there's a line-up to get inside. And that normally spells trouble.

I'm coming, Ellie. I'm coming.

My untied laces act as a hazard as I sprint harder and faster at the sight of the busy bar, but I don't bother to tie them. Even if I fell face first in a pile of snow, I'd have the possibility of Ellie's safety being at risk to pick me straight back up again. I can't afford to have her alone. Not for one second. Not tonight. Not any night.

I reach the front door of the bar. Two bouncers are holding the line of impatient drunks waiting to get inside. A group of guys at the front recognize me and start shouting out for an autograph.

I'm too focused on the bouncers. I work my way around the line of people, finally reaching the front of the line.

"You've got to let me in," I breathe, gripping the biggest bouncer by the jacket. It's a weird feeling being bigger and bulkier than a nightclub bouncer, and I'm sure if it came down to it, I could take both of these fuckers at the same time.

"Miles Johnson?" The bouncer smiles, his eyes bright. A hot breath of steam leaves his smiling mouth as he turns to his buddy and then back to me. "You don't need to wait in line, big guy. Come in!"

He grips the red rope that's blocking the door, unhooks it, and pushes the door of *The Bloody Viking* open. I offer a quick smile as thank you, but there's only one thing I want right now, and that's to find…

"Ellie?"

ALSO BY C.H. JAMES

MORE BOOKS BY C.H. JAMES?

Want more? Yes, please!

Instalove Short Reads:

Curvy Girl Getaway Series

Broken Promise

Spanish Secret

Kiss at Midnight

Rebound Suite

Curvy Girl Getaway Series - The Complete Collection

Curvy Kilts Series

Andrew – My First Love

Robert – My Older Man

The Locker Room Series

My Curvy Puck

Captain's Curvy Puck

Puck My Roommate

My Virgin Puck

The Locker Room Series - The Complete Collection

Operation: Curvy - A Navy SEAL Series

Sealing Her Fate

Operation SEAL Her

Surrender To Her

Her Curvy Explosion

The Falls Creek Falcons - Bad Boys of Falls Creek Series

Bad Boy: SHUT OUT

Bad Boy: GAME OVER

Bad Boy: PRESSURE

Bad Boy: HARD PLAY

ABOUT THE AUTHOR

STEAM. ALPHA. HEA.

INSTALOVE.

Bestselling author C.H. James writes short, spicy, addictive stories. Escape the real world in exotic locations with hot heroes and relatable characters. There is ALWAYS a happily ever after, leaving you satisfied and hungry for more.

A steady stream of new releases will keep you busy, so please follow C.H. James by signing up to the newsletter at: https://b it.ly/chjamesnewsletter